W9-CUD-050

DISCARD

A BROTHER FOR
THE ORPHELINES

Other books by
Natalie Savage Carlson

THE HAPPY ORPHELINE
Pictures by Garth Williams

THE FAMILY UNDER THE BRIDGE
Pictures by Garth Williams

SASHES RED AND BLUE
Pictures by Rita Fava

WINGS AGAINST THE WIND
Pictures by Mircea Vasiliu

THE TALKING CAT
And Other Stories of French Canada
Pictures by Roger Duvoisin

A BROTHER FOR THE ORPHELINES

BY

Natalie Savage Carlson

PICTURES BY

Garth Williams

HARPER & ROW, PUBLISHERS, NEW YORK AND EVANSTON

CARSON LIBRARY
SAN DIEGO CITY SCHOOLS

San Diego, Calif.

A BROTHER FOR THE ORPHELINES

Text copyright © 1959 by Natalie Savage Carlson
Pictures copyright © 1959 by Garth Williams

Printed in the United States of America

All rights in this book are reserved.
No part of the book may be used or reproduced
in any manner whatsoever without written per-
mission except in the case of brief quotations
embodied in critical articles and reviews. For
information address:
Harper & Row, Publishers, Incorporated,
49 East 33rd Street, New York 16, N. Y.

Library of Congress catalog card number: 59–5313

MAR1965

For my granddaughter,
Thela Marie Sullivan,
so she will have her very
own book

A BROTHER FOR
THE ORPHELINES

CHAPTER ONE

Josine was the smallest of the twenty little girls who lived together in a village near Paris. They were all *orphelines*–as the French people call girl orphans.

They were happy orphelines, because they were well treated by Madame Flattot, the woman who ran the orphanage, and Genevieve, the girl who took care of them.

"Brigitte is the happiest of my children and Josine is the stubbornest," Madame Flattot declared.

"Someday Josine's stubbornness will get her somewhere," said Genevieve, because Josine was her favorite since she was the smallest.

"But where will it get her?" sighed Madame Flattot. "Where will it get us all? That is my worry."

Right now Josine's stubbornness was helping her to make a mask for the Mardi gras party that Monsieur de Goupil had promised they should have on the "fat" Tuesday before Lent began. French children celebrate Mardi gras in much the same way that American children do Hallowe'en, only they don't play tricks or go from house to house.

Monsieur de Goupil was in charge of the girls' orphanage and the boys' home on the other side of the village. He tried to keep the orphans happy, too. But he lived alone in Paris so he wasn't always sure exactly what made children happy.

The orphelines were fashioning masks out of paper bags and scraps of cloth. Madame had promised that they might choose costumes from the "charity" trunk in the attic. It was full of old clothes that people had donated to the orphans. There were women's long dresses, sweaters full of holes, blouses with the buttons removed, and even a black evening gown with torn ruffles and loose sequins.

"I'm going to be an Indian of the Far West," decided Josine.

She had once seen a moving picture about American Indians, and she thought that they had lively times.

Genevieve had given her three feathers out of the duster. "And they will have to be enough until some real Indian sends me his war bonnet for dusting the furniture," she said.

Josine was having trouble. The scissors wouldn't cut straight. The eyeholes didn't match. And when she tried to glue the feathers to the mask, they kept sticking to her fingers instead of the paper.

"I'll help you," offered Brigitte, holding up a pretty black lace mask that wouldn't hide her golden earrings.

But Josine pulled her half-finished mask away. "No, Brigitte," she said. "I'm going to make it all by myself. Then if Monsieur de Goupil says I have won the prize for the best mask, it will really belong to me."

Brigitte could understand that because she felt the same way about winning prizes. When Mademoiselle Grignon, their teacher, said, "Brigitte, you have won the medal for composition," she knew she had done the writing all by herself. It made a good feeling inside her.

3

Josine finished her mask by herself, even if one eye-
hole was higher than the other and two feathers were
glued together so they didn't stand up straight. She
colored the face red with a blunt crayon.

The orphelines giggled and chattered as they dressed
in the ragged clothes that some people had thought
would be all right for orphans. How surprised Monsieur
de Goupil would be! He wouldn't know one from the
other when they were masked.

But when Monsieur de Goupil finally arrived in his

new Italian car that looked like a big white egg, he was in no mood for a party.

He didn't even look at the clever masks and costumes. He went stamping around, staring up at the ceilings and thumping the walls.

"The building is in a deplorable condition," he declared. "Deplorable."

"It was only yesterday that we mopped the floors and rubbed down the walls," said Madame Flattot. She was dressed like a Breton woman with a handkerchief gathered into a white coif on her head and her own embroidered shawl over her shoulders.

"This spring has been so rainy that the children have had to play indoors almost every day," explained Genevieve, who hadn't found time to dress like anybody but herself.

This only increased Monsieur de Goupil's complaints. He pointed out the brown stains in a corner of the ceiling.

"The rain surely did that," he said. "The roof must be leaking badly. It will doubtless fall in soon."

The orphelines looked up at the ceiling anxiously.

"I hope it doesn't fall on my rocking chair," said Josine. "One rung is broken already and the back is loose."

5

Monsieur de Goupil only shook his head sadly. Then he insisted on making a complete tour of the rambling building. Everyone followed him, because no one wanted to be alone if the roof fell in. The stairs creaked as so many feet climbed to the attic.

"Probably termites," said Monsieur. "Someday somebody will fall through the steps."

"It won't be me because I don't weigh much," said Josine happily.

"It will probably be Madame Flattot," guessed Brigitte.

The white-coifed woman snorted. "I have outlived many a termite," she scoffed.

The state of the attic disturbed Monsieur de Goupil even more. "That's where the roof is leaking," he pointed. "Several tiles must be gone. But it is scarcely worth reroofing."

He pried into dark corners and crannies. Then he triumphantly pulled out a handful of shredded newspapers. He tossed it over the children's costumes as if it were confetti. "Mice," he said. "The place is infested with mice."

Madame Flattot pulled her scarf tighter over her plump shoulders. "Oh, I know they're getting bad," she said, "but every time I set traps, the dear children

6

are heartbroken. And Josine caught her fingers in one."

"I wanted to see how it felt to be a mouse," explained Josine.

"And we didn't want the poor little mice to be snapped like that," said Brigitte.

"Because Josine cried," added Yvette.

Monsieur de Goupil stalked down the creaking steps. He went out into the courtyard. He pointed at a hole near the bottom of the stone wall. "The wall is crumbling," he said.

"We crumbled it a little," confessed Josine. "Some of the stones were loose, so we pulled them out to see what made them stick together."

"It's only clay," said Brigitte. "No wonder it crumbles."

Then Monsieur de Goupil spotted the worst thing. He pointed to the puddle between the cobbles and the mud tarts "cooking" on a flat rock. "The pipes are leaking," he said. "The rain couldn't make that much mud. The pipes are old and rusty." He turned upon Madame Flattot severely. "The orphanage is a slum," he pronounced.

Madame's temper began to simmer.

"Do you expect me to move the orphelines up in the trees to live with the birds?" she asked testily. "The orphanage has been in this condition for the ten years I have lived in it."

"It will get worse rapidly," said Monsieur gloomily. "The directors will have to do something about it."

"We could camp out in the woods," said Brigitte, because she thought that would be great fun. "We could make houses out of branches and cook our meals over a campfire."

Then Monsieur's mood changed. He smiled and pulled at his ear as if he were quite happy at having found so many things wrong with the orphanage. When he was asked to judge the costumes and pick out the best, he immediately chose Josine's.

"It is a very clever little rooster costume," he smiled. "Very clever."

"I'm not a rooster," Josine corrected him.

"She's an Indian from the Far West," explained Brigitte.

Monsieur cleared his throat. "Ha, very clever!" he repeated and gave Josine a box of bonbons tied with a red ribbon.

Then Madame passed lemonade around and everyone forgot about the roof and steps that might fall in at any minute.

But Monsieur didn't forget the broken pipes.

Next morning three Arab laborers arrived to dig up

the pipes and replace them with new ones. They were dark-skinned sullen men with piercing black eyes and white teeth. Their clothing was ragged and one of them wore a cap made of brown paper. From her work on the mask, Josine knew just how he had made it. He had cut off the top of a paper bag so the round bottom fitted his head just right. Then he had turned up the edge for a brim.

When the orphelines weren't in the classroom studying, they were usually out in the courtyard watching the Arabs work. They tried to talk with the strange men, but they were silent and unfriendly.

"Perhaps they will dig up some diamonds," said Brigitte. "Wouldn't it be grand to have our own diamond mine?"

"Perhaps they will uncover some ancient ruins," said Yvette. "Like those we saw in the museum."

"I wish they'd dig into a rabbit hole," said Josine. "Wouldn't Monsieur be surprised if he found our courtyard full of rabbits?"

But all the Arabs dug up were some rusty pipes and broken stones. Madame thought they weren't working fast enough. The water was shut off for long periods every day. And each day she went out in the courtyard and told the men they would have to work harder and faster. "Why do two of you have to stand around watching the third work?" she asked. "Can't you all work at the same time?"

But the Arabs didn't say any more to her than they had to the children. The orphelines had already lost interest in them. They went about their play, having tea parties in the courtyard and romping through noisy games. The spring weather had changed its mind and turned sunny, so when they weren't in the schoolroom, they played outside. They climbed over the piles of cobblestones. They made mud tarts with the wet dirt loosened by the workmen. They clawed the hole in the wall bigger so they could watch the people going past on the street outside.

The Arab with the paper cap often watched them. He watched when Madame thought he should be digging.

One afternoon when Josine had gone back alone to get her little chair, the Arab slyly beckoned to her. Josine put the chair down and went to him slowly. She was a little frightened, so she didn't go too close.

"You seem so happy here," said the Arab in a low voice.

"We have to be happy here," said Josine. "This is the only place we have to be happy in—even if it is all broken."

The Arab smiled faintly. "Do you get enough to

11

eat?" he asked. "You look plump."

Josine nodded. "Madame and I eat the most of everybody," she said. "One day I ate six chocolate buns."

The Arab leaned on his shovel in the lazy way that
made Madame so angry when the water was turned off.
"Is she the woman who talks to herself?" he asked.

"I never heard her talk to herself," said Josine. "She's
too busy talking to us."

"We do," said the man. "Every day she comes out
and talks at us. But we don't listen, so she is talking to
herself."

"Madame's real nice," said Josine defensively. "She's
our best mother. And Genevieve's our mother, too. She's
lots of fun. Do you have any children?"

"Too many," said the man gloomily.

"Madame says there never could be too many children," said Josine. "She loves us. She even loves me and I'm stubborn."

The Arab rolled his black eyes thoughtfully. Then he went back to shoveling dirt on the new pipes. He refused to speak again. No matter what question Josine asked about his too-many children, he acted as if he had not heard her. So she got tired of talking to herself and carried her chair inside.

The orphelines couldn't get over discussing their deplorable house. "I think it's lovely," said Brigitte indignantly. "We've had so much fun in it."

"If we lived in a new house, we couldn't swing on

the doors or bounce balls on the ceiling, could we?" asked Josine.

"I would be satisfied if only we had running water all day long," said Madame Flattot.

At last Madame was satisfied. The last shovelful of dirt was dropped over the pipes and the last cobblestone set in place. The Arabs swung their shovels and picks over their shoulderrs and departed without a word of farewell. Soon they were completely forgotten.

Madame had her water when she wanted it, but she did not always have the bread on time. One morning the children had to go without bread for breakfast because the bakery boy hadn't come yet. There was a big breadbasket at the bottom of the steps where he left the long loaves if no one answered the gate bell.

"That baker must have forgotten the ovens again," said Madame Flattot impatiently.

The baker often burned the bread, but the woman who ran the bakery couldn't discharge him because he was her husband.

The orphelines had to go to classes that morning without any bread for breakfast. Josine was too young to go to school so she was helping Genevieve dust the furniture. After the Mardi gras party, she had made the three Indian feathers into a little duster of her very own.

"Josine," Madame called from the kitchen, "will you

14

please look again and see if the bread has come yet?"

Josine obediently laid down her feather duster and went running out the door and down the steps. She leaned over the side of the basket. The sight she saw was such a surprise that for a few moments she couldn't move. Then she cried out with excitement. "A baby!" she yelled. "Madame! Genevieve! A baby in our bread-basket!"

The baby was wrapped in a coarse sack with only its head showing–a head full of curly black hair. Josine lifted it into her arms. She carefully climbed the steps sidewise with her heavy burden. It was hard to open the door, but she managed it by supporting the baby against the wall. Then she hurried into the kitchen.

"A dear little baby!" she cried with dancing blue eyes. "The bakery boy left a baby this morning instead of bread."

CHAPTER TWO

Madame Flattot and Genevieve were even more surprised than Josine when they saw the dark-skinned baby with the curly black hair.

"Heaven's mercy!" begged Madame. "I do believe it's an Algerian baby at that."

"I think it's a gypsy," said Genevieve. "See what curly hair she has."

"It's curlier than mine, isn't it?" asked Josine.

"Where did this baby come from?" asked Madame Flattot.

"She was in the breadbasket," said Josine. "Isn't it nice that we got a baby this morning instead of bread? Aren't you glad we waited?"

Madame Flattot was flustered over having a baby arrive in such an unusual way.

"Josine, run out and see if anyone is near the gate," she ordered. "Anyone who looks like the baby's mother."

Josine obeyed willingly. She ran out the door, across the cobbles, and through the open gateway. She looked up and down the narrow street bordered with stone walls. Two soldiers in khaki uniforms with blue caps were walking along the opposite wall. A nun went buzzing by on a motor bicycle with her black veil streaming out behind her. An old lady cautiously shepherded her three dogs across the street.

Josine didn't think that any of them looked like someone who had just abandoned a baby. She hurried back into the house.

"There's nobody out there who looks like a mother," she told Madame Flattot. "May we keep the baby? Oh, please, please may we keep the baby? Oh, please, please may we keep her?"

Madame rocked the dark baby gently in her plump arms. "Oh, I hope that we can," she answered fervently. "I hope they won't send her to the home for foundlings. It has been so long since we've had a baby here. Not since you were a tiny one."

Josine did not like to be reminded of that because she felt very big. Even bigger now that someone younger than herself had appeared at the orphanage.

She divided her time between looking at the new baby and running to the schoolroom door to see if classes were out yet. Wait until all the others found out about this new baby!

After what seemed hours and days, Josine heard a scraping of feet in the schoolroom followed by a babble of voices. She couldn't wait any longer so she opened the door herself.

"You can't guess what got left in our breadbasket this morning," she cried to the orphelines as they left their desks. She began dancing from one foot to the other. "Oh, you'll never guess."

"Bread?" asked Charlotte, who didn't have much of an imagination.

"A cake with chocolate frosting and almonds sliced all over the top?" asked Yvette hopefully.

"Kittens," guessed Brigitte because she thought that nothing else could make Josine so excited.

18

"No, no, no," answered Josine. Then, because the secret was too big to hold any longer, she shouted, "It's a baby. A dear little baby. And maybe we can keep her because the mother doesn't want her any more."

The orphelines were as excited about the baby as Josine. They scampered into the kitchen, pushing and shoving each other. What Josine had told them was true. Madame Flattot was sitting on the kitchen bench with a strange baby in her lap. She had taken off its ragged clothes and wrapped it in a big, soft towel.

"May we keep the baby, Madame?" cried Brigitte. "Oh, please may we keep her? We haven't had a baby since Josine was one."

"And that was an awfully long time ago," Josine reminded them.

"Oh, please let us keep the baby, Madame," cried the others.

But Madame Flattot only looked at them sadly and shook her head. "We cannot keep this sweet little baby, children," she said.

"Why not?" asked Josine with disappointment. "Did her mother come back and say she wants her?"

"Because she is a foundling instead of an orpheline?" asked Brigitte, who knew the difference that made.

Madame Flattot looked unhappier than ever. "Children," she declared firmly, "we cannot keep this baby

19

because it is a *boy*."

The orphelines were stunned into a short silence. Then Josine asked anxiously, "Don't we like boys?"

"What's wrong with boys?" demanded Brigitte.

"There is nothing wrong with boys when they are where they belong," answered Madame. "But that place is not in a girls' orphanage."

Josine had a solution. "Don't tell anybody it's a boy," she begged. "Let's pretend it's a girl."

20

Madame Flattot could not do this. "It would be very wrong for us and for the baby," she said. "Anyway we may not be able to keep him at all. I will have to notify the police and they will try to find the mother. And if they find her, they will make her take care of her baby."

"But she doesn't want him," cried Brigitte. "And we want a brother so much. Even Josine wasn't a brother when she was a baby."

"Please, please, Madame," begged Josine, "help us to keep him."

"I will have to notify the police first," insisted Madame. "That will have to be done to make it legal."

So Madame Flattot called the police. And the orphelines worried and hugged the thin baby and tried to think of ways they could manage to keep him.

Then a stern policeman with a pistol in his holster and a tablet in his hands came to see the baby for himself, just to make sure that Madame hadn't miscounted the children at the orphanage. He began by questioning Josine.

"Aren't you the one who found the baby in the laundry basket?" he asked her.

"It was a breadbasket," interrupted Brigitte.

"Let the child speak for herself," said the policeman to Brigitte in a cross voice. His stern eyes bored into

Josine as if he were trying to make her say that she had put the baby in the basket herself. "Did you see who left the baby?" he demanded.

Josine was frightened by the policeman's questions. But she didn't want him to be able to find a mother to take the baby away.

"It was a woman wearing a Mardi gras mask," said Josine, because she thought it would be very hard to find such a woman.

"She said she was going to China and never coming back," added Brigitte so that the policeman wouldn't even bother looking for her.

The policeman shook his stubby finger at the orphelines. "You are telling lies," he said, "and that is very wicked."

"Now, children," admonished Madame Flattot, "no one saw who left the baby."

"Then maybe it was a woman with a mask," said Josine.

"How do we know if we didn't see her?" asked Brigitte innocently.

Madame Flattot was quite ashamed of the children, and the policeman looked downright angry.

"Bring the baby here," he ordered.

"Tell Genevieve to bring the baby down," Madame told the children. "She is giving it a bottle right now."

All the forty noisy feet clattered up the steps which Monsieur de Goupil expected to cave in at any time.

Madame Flattot waited, nervously playing with her false braid. The policeman beat out a rat-a-tat on his tablet as he impatiently studied the cracks in the wall.

Then there was a noisy scramble of feet coming down the old stairs. Genevieve, carrying the baby, led the group of grinning orphelines. Madame gave a start as she looked at the baby. The red bow from the bonbon box which Josine had won was tied into his curly hair.

"Here it is," said Genevieve. "A little abandoned gypsy girl."

Madame Flattot disagreed with her again. "It looks like an Algerian to me," she said.

The policeman stared at the dark-skinned baby with the red ribbon in its hair. "You are both wrong," he said. "It is a Moor."

"How do you know?" asked Madame Flattot. "I'm sure it is an Algerian."

The policeman frowned at her as if she were a lying child. "Because I spent my military service in Morocco," he said, "so I know a Moor when I see one. I shall make my report that she is a little Moorish girl."

He began writing on his tablet. The orphelines looked at each other. Brigitte began to giggle. Then Yvette snickered into her fist. Soon even Genevieve was gig-

23

gling. Only Josine did not loosen even a smile.

Madame Flattot's face grew red. She pulled at her braid of hair more nervously. "You may all go out and play," she said. "You, too, Genevieve. Take the children outside."

The giggling group was only too happy to leave the presence of the stern policeman. But Josine didn't look happy about anything.

"That policeman told a lie, too," she said indignantly. "And he wrote his lie down on paper. Our baby isn't a girl."

"S-sh!" warned Genevieve. "He thought he was telling the truth."

But Josine was still insulted. "And Madame says he is an Algerian. That's as much a lie as me saying a woman with a Mardi gras mask left him."

"But maybe he is an Algerian," admitted Genevieve. "Sometimes I'm not sure he is a gypsy. His hair is too curly."

But there were even more guesses to be made about the baby.

Of course Monsieur de Goupil had to come in his white egg of a car to have a look at the new child. The orphelines wanted him to have the right kind of a look. Beside the red bow in the hair, they dressed the baby in a frilly, ruffled baby dress that had ribbons on it.

Josine was glad to see her baby dress on somebody else, as it made her feel more grown up.

The children's eyes pleaded with Madame Flattot not to tell Monsieur that the baby was a boy. Madame looked uncomfortable and red and nervous. She pulled so hard at her braid that it came off her head and she had to fasten it in place again.

"Of course it should go to the foundlings' home," she admitted, "but they will only place it with foster parents. And where would you find a better foster mother than I, Monsieur de Goupil?"

Monsieur had to agree. "Children grow like flowers under your hands, Madame Flattot," he said graciously. "This poor little weed will soon be blooming." He peered closely at the baby and said, "Spanish, no doubt."

"I think she's a gypsy," said Genevieve, as if Josine's stubbornness was a catching thing.

"No, she—he—it looks like an Algerian to me," insisted Madame Flattot.

The orphelines began feeling offended at the way the grownups were acting as if the baby were different because he was dark-skinned. "What does it matter what the baby is?" asked Brigitte. "He—she's a child just like us so she needs a home."

Josine understood exactly what Brigitte meant. "He's

not a kitten or a puppy," she said. "He's an us, isn't he, Brigitte?"

Brigitte sharply jabbed Josine with her elbow. "*She* is a girl like us, only *she* is a baby," she explained to Josine in a voice loud enough for Monsieur de Goupil to hear even if he were deaf.

But Monsieur pulled down the corners of his mouth dolefully. "She has entered a world where the ceiling is leaking and the walls are falling in," he said. "I will especially remind the directors that the number of our children keeps growing. But there is no need for me to mention that the newcomer is a foundling. As Brigitte has so cleverly put it, one child is no different from another."

Monsieur said "Bida, bida, bidou" to the beribboned baby. Then he cocked his beret over his right eye and started for the door. Madame followed him unhappily.

"Monsieur," she said in a faint voice, "there is something I must tell you."

"Not now, not now, Madame," said Monsieur de Goupil impatiently. "I am in a great hurry."

"But it is important," persisted Madame.

Monsieur de Goupil gave her moist hand a brisk shake. "Do not worry about the foundling, Madame," he said. "Just find a name for her. Our orphans always

27

enter with a name." Then he smiled brightly as he drove away.

Madame Flattot returned to find Josine holding the baby on her knees. Genevieve was looking puzzled.

"I don't understand Monsieur," said Genevieve. "He actually seems to gloat over the bad state of the house. Yet he is so willing to take another child."

Madame was puzzled, too. "I think that Monsieur is cracking an egg," she stated. "But just what kind of an omelet he plans to make with it remains to be seen."

Josine did not care whether Monsieur de Goupil was going to make an omelet or not. "Coucky, Coucky, Coucky," she sang to a tune she was making up herself. "You're my little Coucky brother."

Madame Flattot gazed at her and the baby lovingly but sadly. "Alas, poor innocents," she said. "Now we are all caught in a web of lies. Oh, what will happen to us?"

"We'll get to keep Coucky," said Josine.

This reminded Madame Flattot that the baby needed a name. "And it will have to be a boy's name," she said. "We must always be truthful and honest."

"His name is Coucky," said Josine. "I made it up myself."

"In our France," said Madame, "a baby cannot be

given a made-up name. And it must be a good French one."

"But I like Coucky," insisted Josine.

"What about Napoleon?" asked Genevieve. "That's a great name, and it's the most French one I know."

"And there was a St. Napoleon," added Madame piously.

"Perhaps he will be St. Coucky," said Josine. "He's such a good baby."

Madame Flattot put her hands on her hips and leaned over Josine.

"If I went to the mayor's office, Josine," she said, "and told him to write in his big book that there is now a baby named Coucky in Ste. Germaine, he would say, 'There is no such name so there is no such baby.'"

"But we could bring Coucky and show him to the mayor," insisted Josine stubbornly.

Genevieve had an idea. "Each of you could take a slip of paper and write down the name you want for the baby. Then the name with the most votes will win."

"I want somebody to write down the name Coucky for me," said Josine.

"There's no such name, so nobody will write it for you," said Yvette.

Josine gave the baby to Madame. She went over by the

29

door and sat down on the bench. She swelled her lips in a pout. Genevieve tore a sheet of paper into enough pieces. Some pencils were brought from the schoolroom and the girls began chewing on them and rolling the edges of the paper as they tried to think of good names. Names good enough for such a precious baby as a new brother.

After quite a long time of thinking, the last mind was made up and the last name written. Only Josine did not have to think about a name, because she had chosen hers before, although no one would write it for her.

Genevieve and Madame Flattot began going through the names and sorting them. There were four Jeans and three Pierres and even an Alexandre, but there were eleven Napoleons.

"So Coucky will be named Napoleon," said Madame. "And his last name can be Lepetit since that is 'the little one.' "

Brigitte tried to soothe Josine. "That will be a beautiful name for Coucky," she said.

"I bet Coucky will be proud of it when he gets big," added Yvette.

So the little dark-skinned baby was named Napoleon Lepetit in the mayor's big book. But for some strange reason he was never called anything but Coucky.

CHAPTER THREE

It looked as if the orphelines might get to keep Coucky. Of course Madame Flattot kept squeezing her hands together and saying that she would have to make a full confession to Monsieur de Goupil. But the policeman didn't come back, so it seemed the baby's mother was still lost. And the mayor didn't care if the Napoleon Lepetit in his big book lived in a girls' orphanage or an old soldiers' home.

Josine had claimed Coucky for her very own from the start. She helped Genevieve bathe him and give him his bottle. They gave him bottles so often that he was soon plump and happy.

Josine played a little game with him which French mothers play with their babies. She would lightly touch his curly black hair. "The garden," she would say.

She would tap his forehead then point to his eyes. "The path, the lamps," she called them in turn. His nose, his mouth, and his hands were the gutters, the oven, and the drumsticks.

When she said "drumsticks," she grabbed his tiny wrists between her fingers and she made his little hands lightly drum his round, fat stomach. "The drum," she ended. "Beat the drum! Zim la boum! Zim la boum!" Then the baby would gurgle with delight and kick his legs at her.

Madame Flattot and Genevieve used their own money to buy Coucky some new baby clothes.

"It is bad enough for a boy to be in a girls' orphanage, without having to wear their cast-off baby clothes," said Madame. "If he were my own little boy, I would want him to have new clothes."

So because she felt as if every child in the orphanage were her own, she bought Coucky a plain white dress and a blue blanket with a white lamb on it.

Genevieve knit him a woolly cap and a blue sweater.

"But he will have to use the old baby carriage in the attic," said Madame. "It is really quite sturdy."

Josine objected to this, but not because it was second-hand. "It's too heavy for me to push far," she told Madame. "I wish he could have a little carriage like the *poussette* you push to market when you don't buy much."

"Why not the *poussette?*" asked Genevieve. "We could fix it up comfortably for the baby. Then Josine could push him in the park and around the block some-times."

The *poussette* was a low basket on four wheels with a slender handle that was just right for Josine if she grasped it at the sides. Genevieve made a soft pillow and padded the inside.

"It needs some kind of a shade to keep the sun off the baby," she decided.

"That blue lampshade in the parlor would be just the thing," said Madame Flattot. "It has such beautiful tassels all around the edge."

"We could wire it in place," added Genevieve.

"Oh, please let me help," begged Josine. "Please let me do something."

So they let her go to the hardware store with Brigitte to ask the owner if he had any wire that would bend easily, but not too easily.

At last the *poussette* was a baby carriage. The orphelines gazed at it ecstatically and clasped their hands.

"It doesn't look like any other baby carriage in the world," said Brigitte.

"It doesn't even look like a *poussette* any more," said Genevieve.

Josine thought that pushing Coucky in the *poussette* was the most fun in all the world. The wheels rattled, the basket shook, and the tassels on the lampshade waved back and forth elegantly.

Even when Genevieve took the orphelines on a tour of the sewers of Paris, Josine wanted to stay home and push Coucky around the block in his new-old *poussette.*

Since the children had taken such an interest in the repairing of the pipes under the cobblestones, Madame Flattot thought they would enjoy going on the conducted tour of the sewers.

"It is all very clean," she explained to them. "Paris is proud of its sewers. Even people from other countries go to see them as well as the art treasures in the Louvre."

"You will go down right under the pavement and sail on an underground canal," promised Genevieve, who had once taken the tour with her godmother.

"It will be very educational," said Madame Flattot, "so listen carefully to the guide when he tells you how many liters of water are used in Paris daily and how many kilometers of pipes carry it underground."

Josine was torn between the *poussette* and the underground boat ride.

"If I go," she said to Madame Flattot, "you'll take good care of Coucky, won't you? You won't drop him or forget to feed him?"

"Have I ever dropped one of you or forgotten to feed her?" asked Madame testily.

35

But when the girls were all ready to leave for the autobus, Coucky began to squall lustily.

"Oh, I can't leave him," said Josine, pulling off her cloak and hood. "All the time I would wonder if he was still crying."

So she wistfully watched the other orphelines marching down the street in rows, holding hands.

She was tempted to cry out, "Wait for me! I want to go after all." But her stubbornness wouldn't let her.

"I promised Coucky I would stay with him," she told Madame Flattot. "Babies certainly tie you down, don't they?"

Josine spent the afternoon wheeling the *poussette* around in the courtyard, but to her chagrin Coucky kept on crying.

Madame and she did everything they could to make him comfortable. But he was most ungrateful and howled until his face was red as the ribbon he had worn for the policeman and Monsieur de Goupil.

Josine wished she had gone on the tour with the others. The afternoon seemed to last forever. She even grew bored pushing the *poussette*, and cut out paper dolls for a while.

At last the girls came back, their eyes bright and their cheeks rosy.

"It was like the *Enchanted River* ride in the Bois de Bologne," cried Brigitte, "only it was under the ground and it smelled like dishwater."

"We sailed under Paris," said Marie. "We were even under the Seine River one time."

"There were lots of boats and they all had big lights on them," added Yvette. "And men pulled them with chains."

"We played we were goblins and that our boat was full of rubies and emeralds we had dug out of the earth," said Brigitte.

But no one remembered how many liters of water were used in Paris each day nor how many kilometers of pipe carried it.

Josine listened with a pang at her heart. If only she had been there to play goblin, too.

And that evening when Coucky wouldn't drink his milk and kept wriggling between her knees, she said to him, "Sometimes I think you aren't worth giving up a sewer for."

But Madame Flattot was having suspicions about Coucky's bad humor. She pushed her finger into his mouth and ran it along his gums.

"Aha!" she cried triumphantly. "It is just as I suspected. He is making himself a tooth."

"Oh, my poor baby," cried Josine sympathetically. "If I hadn't stayed with him, he would have had to make his tooth all alone."

They all loved him so much that they worried and worried about his tooth.

One night Josine woke up to hear him crying. His complaints came faintly across the hallway. Josine was afraid that Madame Flattot would sleep through his crying and wouldn't do anything for him.

She crawled out of bed. She felt her way to the door and opened it. She was half asleep and almost lost in the dark. Somehow she made the wrong turn in the hall. Her feet stepped into nothingness. She went falling into a dark pit.

Josine grabbed for something but only succeeded in knocking Madame Flattot's bowl of house plants off the niche. Bump, bump, bump went Josine down the steps and crack, clatter, clink went the bowl of plants. All the way to the bottom of the steps they went.

Josine thumped to a stop. Then she began wailing loudly because she was frightened and bruised and everything was so black.

Above her own crying, she heard a commotion upstairs. There was a sound of scurrying feet and a faint gleam of light. Doors squeaked open.

She heard Madame Flattot's voice scream, "Heaven's mercy on us! The roof has caved in on the children."

Genevieve's voice was high-pitched. "The noise was in the hallway," it cried. "The stairs have fallen in."

Then Brigitte shrieked. "They fell on Josine," she squealed. "I hear her crying and she isn't in her bed."

The hallway light was switched on. Josine stopped crying. She whimpered, "The stairs didn't fall on me. I fell on them." She felt the broken bits of pottery around her. "And I'm all broken into little pieces."

Madame Flattot rushed down the stairs and lifted Josine into her arms. She carried her back. She led the ghostly parade to the sickroom, with its shelves of bottles and basins.

It turned out that Josine wasn't broken into little pieces. She was only frightened and bruised. There was a tiny cut from the broken bowl on her arm. Madame put a bandage on the cut and rubbed the bruises with some medicine, but they didn't stop hurting until Genevieve kissed them. The bowl was too broken to be put together by medicine or kisses.

As for Coucky, he had peacefully fallen asleep during the din.

Madame Flattot ran her fingers through her hair, which was so thin because the braid was lying on her bureau. "Monsieur will have to do something about that roof and those stairs," she vowed.

"But they didn't really fall in," Genevieve reminded her.

"We thought they had because Monsieur warned us about them," said Madame. "That's what frightened us most, so they will have to be fixed. Another night like this would kill me."

"It might kill me, too," said Josine.

Monsieur de Goupil drove out from Paris at Madame's urgent request. He looked happy as a wedding

cake because Madame Flattot had been frightened by the roof and the stairs even though they hadn't actually fallen on anyone.

"It is not my fault, Madame," he said. "I am doing everything I can. I have a truly brilliant idea, but I can't convince the directors."

Madame Flattot waited to hear his brilliant idea, but he seemed to want to keep it a secret. Then, because her conscience was worrying her as much as the roof and the stairs, she said to him, "I have a confession to make, Monsieur."

"Is something else wrong?" asked Monsieur de Goupil pleasantly.

"I am wrong," said Madame. "I have been sheltering a boy under this leaky roof."

"A boy!" exclaimed Monsieur in a shocked voice. "A boy in a girls' orphanage!"

"It's Coucky," said Madame. "She is really a boy."

Monsieur de Goupil put his hands to his head and groaned.

"Now that we have made him an orphan instead of a foundling," he said, "we are in a hot pot of soup. Our only way out is to send him to the boys' home. And it is already overcrowded."

Madame Flattot regained hope. "If it's too crowded," she said, "he might as well stay here."

"No, that would never do," said Monsieur de Goupil. "Put on your coat and we will take the baby over there right away."

"Oh, no, no," cried Madame in distress. "We can't. It isn't possible."

Monsieur was impatient. "And why isn't it possible?" he wanted to know.

"It's impossible," maintained Madame Flattot, "be-cause—because—because he's making a tooth."

"Can't he make his tooth at the boys' orphanage?" asked Monsieur de Goupil.

"Oh, dear, no," said Madame desperately. "Alas, no! It would upset him to make the change at this time. It would upset all the children."

Monsieur grudgingly gave in. "But after he has made his tooth," he threatened, "he will have to go to the boys' home where he belongs."

CHAPTER FOUR

On Easter morning all the orphelines went to the church with the cock on its high spire. They wore new dresses of blue and white polka dot silk. Coucky couldn't go to church, but he was promenaded through the park that afternoon so everyone could see how handsome he looked in the cap and jacket that Genevieve had knit. And that gave the orphelines another chance to show off their polka dot dresses.

Then Coucky celebrated his own Easter by cutting his tooth all the way through the gum.

That worried the orphelines at first, but he immediately began cutting another tooth. So Madame Flattot could truthfully tell Monsieur de Goupil that he was still making teeth and couldn't possibly be moved to the boys' orphanage yet.

But one beautiful spring morning, all the orphelines ran up to the attic, where Josine was putting out crumbs for the mice.

"Coucky's mother has come for him," they shouted. "She's down in the parlor with Madame and she's wearing her Mardi gras mask. She wants to see you."

Josine was surprised that Coucky's mother had turned out the way she had described her. But she was horrified to hear that she had come for her baby.

She went running down the stairs so fast that she nearly fell down them again. But there was no one in the parlor with Madame Flattot. She was alone, dusting the pictures.

The orphelines burst out laughing.

"Fish Day," cried Yvette. "Josine is an April fish."

"Josine swallowed the bait," cried Marie. "It's the first day of April."

French children celebrate the first of April like Americans, only they call it the Day of the Fish instead of April Fools' Day.

"Now you shouldn't play the joke on Josine," scolded Madame Flattot, "because she is so little."

"I'm glad it was a joke," said Josine thankfully. "I'm glad Coucky's mother didn't really come to take him away."

Coucky did not seem to want to leave the girls either. When the first day of May arrived, he was still cutting teeth.

"May we go to the woods again this year to pick lilies of the valley?" Brigitte asked Madame Flattot.

The first of May is Lily-of-the-Valley Day in France. People gather the flowers in the woods and give sprigs to their friends for good luck. Even the president of France gets one, because ever since the days of King Louis IX, the head of the French government has been presented with a lily of the valley on the first of May.

"But of course," said Madame Flattot. "Genevieve will take you to the Ste. Germaine woods. We need all the good luck we can get even if we have to gather it ourselves."

Josine was anxious. "May we take Coucky, too?" she asked. "He needs the most good luck of everybody."

Madame Flattot agreed. "An outing in the woods would be good for him," she said.

So Coucky was bundled into his *poussette* and Josine was allowed to push him.

The girls marched ahead in rows, hand in hand.

Brigitte had even made a banner to carry by spearing a piece of tinfoil on a stick. Josine walked in back with Genevieve, who took a turn pushing the *poussette* when the cobbles were unusually rough or the curb high.

They went past the empty market place and down a street where people hid their houses behind high stone walls. They met the main road at the woods and followed it on the bicycle path.

The trees were wearing new leaves, and men in blue aprons were sweeping up the dead winter ones on the ground. The orphelines ran here and there, looking for the slim green leaves and the little white bells of the lilies of the valley.

Brigitte had the sharpest eyes, so she was gathering the biggest bunch. Then one of the sweepers showed Josine where a great clump of them grew in a thicket.

Each child gave Genevieve a spray for good luck. She pinned a pretty corsage to her rough tweed coat with one of Coucky's safety pins. Each child laid two sprays in Coucky's *poussette*, because he needed luck so much —even more than the president of France.

The orphelines and Genevieve weren't the only people in the woods. Others were tramping over the wet leaves.

Two women went galloping down the path on horseback. Their stylish mounts had been clipped closely all over except for their legs, so that they shone in two shades of chestnut.

Another woman sat on a chair she had brought with her, knotting a market bag from string handily tied to the trunk of a small tree.

Then gay, catchy music came to the ears of the orphelines.

"A merry-go-round," cried Brigitte. "I hear a merry-go-round."

The orphelines clutched their lilies of the valley and went running toward the sound. Josine jiggled the *poussette* over the path as fast as its wheels would turn.

When they came to the edge of the woods, they saw the merry-go-round. It stood near the road, with a brown truck and a green gypsy-like van parked beside it.

Other children had found the merry-go-round first. They were gleefully whirling around to the happy tune. The merry-go-round did not have many horses or animals on it. There were midget autocars and motorcycles and even a tiny train engine for children to ride. There was a swan pulling a cart and an airplane that went up and down. But the thing that caught Josine's eyes was a tiny blue coach drawn by two white horses.

"Oh, I wish Coucky and I could ride in that coach," said Josine.

Genevieve looked ashamed. "I don't have any francs with me to pay for the rides," she said. "All I have in my pocket is the card that proves I'm myself and some safety pins and a letter to mail. But we can watch the merry-go-round."

So the orphelines crowded around it in a half circle.

The stocky, bushy-haired man who owned the merry-go-round saw the eager children.

"Come, come," he called. "Have a ride on my merry-go-round. Twenty francs a ride. Only twenty francs. Get your tickets."

"Not today," replied Genevieve. "We have come to the woods to gather lilies of the valley."

Brigitte was more direct.

"We can't ride the merry-go-round because we haven't any money," she said. She tried to look as piti-ful as possible. "We are poor little orphelines," she said sadly.

Josine helped her. "We live in a slum with broken walls and mice," she added.

Then the man smiled and beckoned to them.

"You shall ride free," he declared. "I was once a poor, unhappy child myself."

"Were you an orphan?" asked Genevieve.

"Worse," said the man glumly. "I was raised by a cruel stepfather. He worked me in the fields from morning to night with hardly enough bread to glue my bones together."

"How dreadful!" exclaimed Genevieve. "We love our children and they are well fed."

The man's dark eyes grew dreamy. "But whenever I felt too miserable," he continued, "I would say to myself, 'Never mind, Lucien. When you are a big man you shall have a merry-go-round.' And you can see that I have."

"How wonderful!" sighed Brigitte.

"I bet you ride it all day long," said Josine.

The man ruefully shook his head. "It was exciting at first," he admitted, "but to tell you the truth, I'm sick of my merry-go-round. I wish the carnival man had never sold it to me so cheap."

"Then why don't you sell it to someone else?" asked Genevieve.

The man looked shocked. "How can I sell the merry-go-round that I promised to a poor, unhappy boy?" he asked her.

Genevieve and the orphelines agreed that he could not possibly break faith with the little boy, even though it had been himself.

ity Schools Library
San Diego, Calif.

The merry-go-round came to a stop and the orphelines jumped aboard before the other children had time to get off. They swooped back and forth like starlings perching in the treetops. First Brigitte straddled a frog, but then she decided she would rather go up and down on the airplane. Marie wanted to ride in the engine, but Yvette was already there, so she had to climb on a motorcycle.

Only Josine had no trouble, because her mind had been made up from the first.

"Coucky wants to ride in the blue coach, too," she told Genevieve.

So Genevieve carried the baby while Josine settled herself inside the coach. Then Coucky was pushed into her lap.

The baby gurgled and completely forgot about his tooth as the music played and the coach went around and around. Josine did not care if the coach wasn't going anywhere in particular. She waved to Genevieve each time it went past the place where she was standing.

The orphelines clung to their mounts or vehicles and squealed with delight. They could not imagine anyone ever getting sick of a merry-go-round. But after the third ride, Josine thought that perhaps she was getting sick of it. She felt as if it were going around and around in her stomach. She grew dizzy. She wasn't sure that

she could hold Coucky much longer. She wanted Genevieve to take her off, but she was afraid to open her mouth because of what might happen.

Genevieve saw her white face and called to the merry-go-round man to stop it. She stepped aboard and hurried to Josine. The merry-go-round man ran to her, too.

Genevieve took Coucky and the merry-go-round man helped Josine off.

"Come into my van and lie down on the bed for a while," he suggested to Josine.

He helped her up the steps of the house on wheels. In the very back of it was a soft bed covered with a pieced quilt. On one side was a table with one chair and on the other a tiny stove. Lace curtains hung in the windows and there were brightly papered shelves lining the walls.

The house on wheels was so cute that Josine couldn't stay sick long. Then the man gave her a bottle of lemonade to drink and a stale cookie to eat, although Genevieve did not think these were the best things for a child who had been sick on a merry-go-round.

When Josine felt like herself again instead of a butterfly, Genevieve thanked the man for the tenth time and Josine presented him with a lily of the valley for good luck.

Then Genevieve gathered the orphelines together and counted them and headed them for home.

Josine insisted that she was quite well enough to push the *poussette*.

"Oh, I do hope that Madame will not blame me for letting Josine ride the merry-go-round so long," said Genevieve. "Now hurry, girls! We must get home before our flowers wilt."

Josine had been thinking about something other than lilies of the valley.

"Genevieve," she asked, "would you rather have a million francs and live in a beautiful castle or be poor and have all of us?"

Genevieve took a firm hold of the *poussette's* handle. "If you don't let me push it for a while," she threatened, "I will take the million francs and go off to live in the castle."

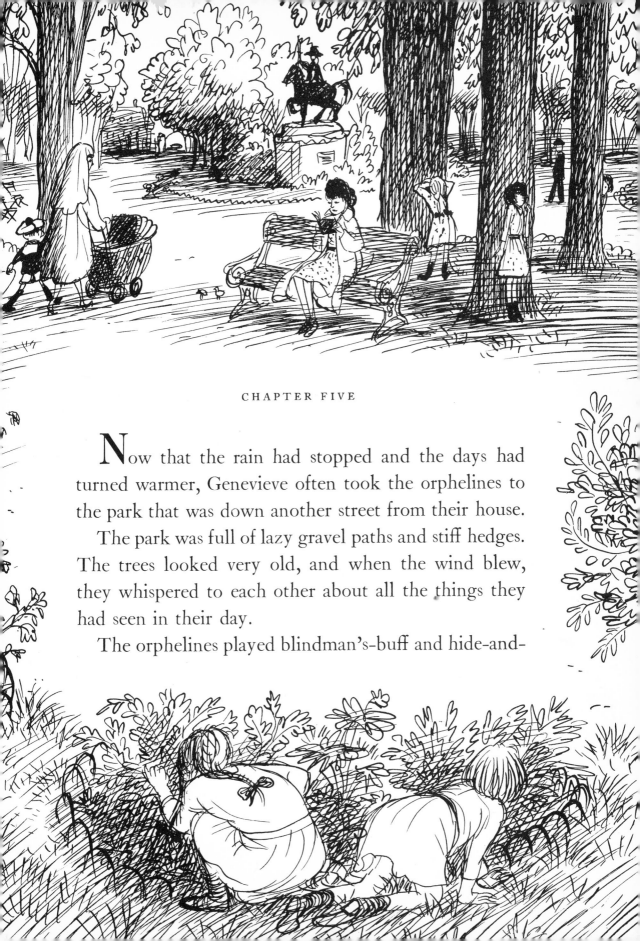

CHAPTER FIVE

Now that the rain had stopped and the days had turned warmer, Genevieve often took the orphelines to the park that was down another street from their house.

The park was full of lazy gravel paths and stiff hedges. The trees looked very old, and when the wind blew, they whispered to each other about all the things they had seen in their day.

The orphelines played blindman's-buff and hide-and-seek and other games in the park while Genevieve sat on a bench and knitted a blanket for Coucky.

Josine liked to wheel the baby down the gravel path and pretend that his *poussette* was a blue coach and she a white horse. The *poussette* creaked, the fringe waved, and often people stopped to admire the dark-skinned baby.

Josine pushed the *poussette* around a clump of rhodo-dendrons. She was glad that she had taken this path. There in a sandy patch of playground was a crowd of boys all dressed alike in blue shorts and blue and white sweaters. Some of them were crouched on their knees around a circle drawn in the sand. They were playing marbles.

She pushed the *poussette* close to the boys. She stood and watched them silently for a few minutes.

"Are you an orphan?" she asked a tall boy whose hair grew in a cowlick.

The boy shrugged his shoulders. "Who isn't?" he asked without interest. "Your turn, Pierre."

The boy named Pierre dropped on his bare knee at the edge of the circle, and the boy with the cowlick went over to watch him.

Josine pushed the *poussette* closer.

"I'm an orpheline," she said to anyone who would

listen to her. "We live in a slum with mice and rusty pipes. But the pipes are fixed now."

A tall freckle-faced boy looked at her. "Pouf!" he scoffed. "Girls would have mice. We have rats."

"They're in the attic," added the boy with the cowlick. "But soon they'll be down with us, because the roof is going to fall in. That's what Monsieur de Goupil says."

"Our roof is going to fall in, too," said Josine proudly. "It almost did the other night and Madame Flattot was awfully scared."

"We don't care," said the boy called Pierre, after he had finished his turn. "We're going to move to a big castle in the country."

"Oh, no, we aren't," the freckle-faced boy corrected him. "The directors won't let us."

Then the boys went on with their marble game. In the French way, they tossed their marbles instead of shooting them with their thumbs. Josine saw that some of their marbles were really steel ball bearings. She knew what they were because she had once seen the bakery boy fixing his bicycle wheel.

"I wish I could play with you," she said.

The boys did not seem to hear her. She raised her voice and addressed herself to Coucky. "I wish those boys would let me play with them," she said.

The boy with the cowlick finished his turn and pocketed the marbles and ball bearings he had won.

Josine spoke even louder to Coucky. "If they would only let me play one game, I wouldn't beg any more," she said.

"Girls don't know how to play marbles," said the boy with the cowlick.

"Don't they?" asked Josine with surprise.

"Oh, let the little gosling play," said the boy with freckles.

"She hasn't any marbles," said a boy with his front teeth missing.

"I'll give her some of my ball bearings," said the freckled boy. "I'll win them back." He turned to Josine. "You know when they're gone you can't play any more."

Josine eagerly took the tiny steel balls in her fist. The boys made her put four of them in the circle. She impatiently awaited her turn. The boy with the missing teeth showed her where to squat.

"You try to knock as many marbles as you can out of the circle," he coached her. "Then they're yours."

Josine nodded. "I like that blue one," she said.

The boys snickered. Josine drew an imaginary line

58

with her eye. She tossed the ball bearing. It rolled into the circle and cracked against the blue marble. Both marble and ball bearing rolled out of the circle. Josine jumped up and quickly pocketed them.

"Did you ever play marbles before?" asked the freckled boy suspiciously.

Josine shook her head. She watched the other boys take their turns. When her own came again, she knocked three marbles out of the circle.

"Don't aim at the marbles," cried the boy with the front teeth missing. "Try to hit the ball bearings. You can put them in the wheels of your baby cart, then it will roll easier."

"I like marbles better," said Josine. She pointed at the *poussette*, where Coucky was gurgling in the sunshine. "When Coucky gets big, will you let him play marbles with you?" she asked. "He's going to live at your home because he's a boy."

The boys immediately forgot their marble losses.

"A baby!" exclaimed the one without front teeth. "We don't want a baby living in our house. We've got enough wrong with it already."

"Monsieur de Goupil says he has to live with you," insisted Josine.

The freckled boy was indignant. "We'd rather have

rats," he exclaimed. "You'll have to take care of the baby, Marcel," he teased the youngest boy, who wasn't much bigger than Josine.

The little fellow scowled darkly. "You better not send any baby to our home," he threatened. "Something awful might happen to him."

"Your Coucky wouldn't like it there," said the freckled boy, winking at Pierre. "They beat us every day and starve us and work us like donkeys, don't they, Pierre?"

"Sure," said Pierre. He pulled up his sleeve and showed Josine a scratch on his arm. "That's where Monsieur Roger beat me," he told her.

Another boy smirked and pointed to his skinned knee. "And that's where he hit me," he said.

Josine was shocked. "But Coucky is only a little baby," she said. "They wouldn't hurt him."

"Monsieur Roger would," Pierre assured her. "He's a toad."

The boys would have gone on telling Josine about Monsieur Roger's cruelty, but one of them called their attention to the marbles. "She's got my best marble," he whined. "She has to put it in next time so I can win it back."

So they played another game, but Josine flatly refused

to put the marble in the circle, and when it was her turn, she won another boy's best marble.

"Are you sure you've never played marbles before?" asked the boy.

Josine innocently shook her head.

Then Genevieve's voice came twittering through the bushes like a bird call. "Josi-i-ine!" it trilled. "Josi-i-ine!"

Josine rattled the marbles and ball bearings in her pocket. "That's Genevieve calling me," she explained.

"You can't go yet," cried a boy in anguish. "You've still got my marbles."

"Josi-i-ine!" came Genevieve's call, growing closer.

The little *orpheline* hurried to the *poussette* and started to turn it around. "Good-by," she cried to the boys.

"Don't go yet," implored the freckled boy. "Give us a chance to win our marbles back. You can keep the ball bearings."

The biggest boy blocked her path. "You have too played marbles before," he accused her.

Josine shook her curls more vigorously than ever. "We didn't have any marbles," she said. "We play the game with nuts. It's harder to make them go straight, but I can beat everybody but Genevieve."

Perhaps the boys would not have let Josine get away

with their marbles if Genevieve and Brigitte hadn't come around the rhododendrons. At sight of them, the biggest boy stepped back. Josine wheeled Coucky up the path to meet Genevieve and Brigitte.

The orphelines were delighted at sight of all the marbles and ball bearings Josine had won.

"Oh, I wish we knew those boys better," said Brigitte. "I wish we could play games with them."

Then Josine told them all the terrible things she had heard about the boys' orphanage. "And there's a mean toad there that will hurt Coucky," she ended.

No one believed her.

"The boys were teasing you," said Genevieve.

But Josine was sure that the boys had told the truth because her own ears had heard the stories. She felt all alone with her worries for Coucky. She would have to be the one to save him from the toad.

Then she thought of someone else who might believe her and realize Coucky's danger. The merry-go-round man! She would go to him and ask him to be Coucky's foster father since the baby was really a foundling.

She decided to go to the merry-go-round in the woods all by herself before supper. So while Coucky was napping and the girls were helping Madame Flattot string beans, Josine started forth.

She couldn't go out the gate because Madame Flattot always kept it locked now so that no more babies could be left in the breadbasket.

"It isn't that we don't want the little innocents," she had explained, "but this is an orphanage, not a foundling home."

Josine went to the hole in the wall. She thought that if she pulled out some more rocks, she could crawl through it.

She got down on her knees and loosened two more rocks. With grunts and puffs, she was able to get them out and make the hole larger. She was sure that she could get through it now.

By holding her breath, she was able to get her shoulders through. Now her head was on the street side, so she could see people coming home from work. She pulled herself harder and pushed with her feet, which were still inside the courtyard. But her plump middle would not go through. Even when she let all the air out of her lungs and pulled her hardest, she couldn't go any farther.

She decided to crawl back inside and pull out some more rocks. But she couldn't push the other way either. Her middle wouldn't move either way. The wall began to feel tight.

Josine began to cry. She cried louder and louder.

A woman coming home with a bagful of long loaves of bread was the first one to see Josine.

"Tata, little one!" exclaimed the woman. "What are you doing in that wall?"

"Trying to get out," wailed Josine. "I'm stuck. The wall won't let go of me."

The woman first tried to pull her out into the street. Then she tried to push her back into the courtyard. But she was no better at it than Josine had been.

At last the woman went running around the corner to the gate so she could arouse someone in the orphanage. "Now don't move," she cried to Josine over her shoulder. "Don't move until I get back."

Josine didn't.

Madame Flattot went scurrying around outside to talk to Josine's head. Genevieve ran into the courtyard to pull Josine's plump legs.

"The wall has fallen on Josine," cried Brigitte. "Are you alive, Josine?" Then she had to run all the way out the gate, which was now unlocked, and around the corner to hear what Josine's mouth had to say about it.

A crowd of people gathered. Each one had a different idea for getting Josine out of the wall. But since the child was howling so loudly by this time, they all agreed that the fire department should be called because she might suffocate.

The fire truck arrived, playing its musical siren. All the firemen wanted to put out a fire, but Genevieve insisted that they must pull a child out of a wall.

The firemen acted disappointed over their job. They

looked at their axes and hoses sadly. Then they studied Josine's predicament.

"This is work for a stonemason," said the chief fireman. "The wall must be taken down stone by stone. If

we loosen the stones around her, the whole wall might cave in on the child."

Someone ran for the stonemason and someone else ran for a chocolate bun to comfort Josine.

But Josine had to be fed two more buns before the stonemason arrived. He was grumbling because he had been taken away from his supper.

"If the child could get into it," he growled, "why can't she get herself out of it?"

"It is the nature of children to get themselves into places they can't get out of," said the chief fireman. "We've pulled children out of pipes and wheels and caves."

It was almost dark by the time Josine was freed from the wall by the stonemason. He had to pry off the rocks from top to bottom. By the time Josine could stand up on her stiff legs, there was a great gap in the rock wall. Josine rubbed her bruises as she looked at it.

"If that had been there before," she said, "I wouldn't have gotten stuck."

CHAPTER SIX

Madame Flattot took Josine to the sickroom again.
As she couldn't find any cuts or broken bones, she gave
the little orpheline a tonic for her appetite and a cough
drop.

"How did you ever get caught in the wall?" she asked.

Josine, in disappointment at her failure, told Madame
everything. She was trying to get out so she could go

to the merry-go-round man and ask him to take Coucky.

"He said he was an unhappy child, so I know he would help us," said Josine. "I thought of it all by myself. Brigitte didn't help me or Yvette or Marie or anybody."

Madame Flattot was displeased.

"It is your stubbornness, Josine," she said. "It is not a little girl's place to try to solve such a big problem by herself. That is what Monsieur de Goupil and Genevieve and I are for." Something else bothered Madame. "You have been a naughty girl, Josine," she continued, "so I shall have to punish you."

Madame twisted her braid and her brain for a punishment which would not hurt Josine but would teach her a lesson.

"It is no longer the style to spank children," she told Genevieve, "and I am just as glad. But Josine must be punished severely."

Genevieve helped Madame to think of a severe punishment which would not be too hard on Josine.

"If she had to wear a sign on her back for tonight and all of tomorrow," said Genevieve, "it would fasten the lesson in her mind. I could make a big sign saying, 'I will never be stubborn again.'"

"That is a splendid idea, Genevieve," agreed Madame,

"but we must not try to work a miracle with pencil and paper. What about 'I will not leave the courtyard without permission'?"

"Perhaps that would be better," said Genevieve. "Especially since the wall is open now."

"I like that one best, too," said Josine. "I don't think I could do the other one."

So Genevieve lettered a large piece of paper with the good resolution which was to be Josine's. She pinned it to the back of her plaid apron.

Josine was disappointed because the sign was on her back, where she couldn't see it, so Genevieve had to make another one to pin on front of her apron.

The little orpheline insisted on learning the words by heart because she couldn't read them. "I don't sound like me at all, do I?" she asked brightly.

Monsieur de Goupil had to be told about Josine's latest wrongdoing. He came to the orphanage next day. He read Josine's signs and looked at the gap in the wall. He clucked his lips.

"It will be a hopeless task," he sighed. "Hopeless!"

"Oh, I think Josine will obey," said Madame Flattot. "She is really proud of her signs."

"It isn't the child I am thinking about," said Monsieur de Goupil. "It's those stubborn directors. I wish I could pin some signs on them. They have decided that the orphanages are to be repaired."

"Isn't that what the buildings need?" asked Madame Flattot sharply.

"It will be a hopeless task," repeated Monsieur de Goupil. "They are too far gone. And where will we find laborers? The Arabs are working on the roads now, and one of them has returned to Algeria because his family is too big for France."

"What about your brilliant idea?" asked Madame, because she was unduly curious about it.

"It is gone, crushed, ended," said Monsieur with a heavy sigh. "But even my brother-in-law, the Duke, agreed that it was truly a brilliant idea."

Again Madame Flattot waited in vain to hear the idea, but it truly seemed gone, crushed, and ended because Monsieur did not divulge it.

Monsieur de Goupil had another matter to settle. "The abandoned boy must go to the house where he belongs," he said. "If he hasn't made all his teeth, Monsieur Roger will help him with the rest. He is growing fast."

"Yes," admitted Madame Flattot. "He is pushing like a mushroom."

"I'm going to the boys' home now," said Monsieur, "so I'll make arrangements for them to receive him Monday. That will start a fresh week."

"But that is only the day after tomorrow," cried Madame. She did not feel that she could think of a new excuse for keeping Coucky in such a short time.

Sunday was a blue day for the girls. They went to church and prayed and prayed that some miracle would save Coucky from the boys' orphanage.

When they came back, Madame put on her hat with the imitation bird perched on the brim. "I am going over to have a little talk with Monsieur Roger," she said.

The orphelines played with Coucky until it was time for him to take his afternoon nap in the courtyard. Then they went to work on their books for the next day's class. Everything seemed peaceful so Genevieve, whose sorrow had turned into a headache, went up to her room to lie down.

Josine sat on the steps in the courtyard, her eyes blurred with tears. She stared at the baby sleeping in his *poussette*. Then she stared at the opening in the wall. Lastly she stared at the front of her Sunday dress.

"I don't have the signs on me any more," she told the sleeping baby, "so now I can take you to the merry-go-round man. If I still had the signs pinned on, I would have to ask Genevieve for permission."

Josine took firm hold of the *poussette's* handle and pushed the carriage through the jagged hole. She wheeled it over the cobbles. Down the street of un-friendly walls, she pushed Coucky.

Again she took the bicycle path that was smooth and shaded. Coucky woke up and began talking to himself. A family was picnicking by the crossroads. They had brought their table and chairs. They sat eating off a white cloth with a vase of freshly picked flowers in the center as neatly and comfortably as if they were home.

"When our house falls down, we'll have a dining room like that," Josine told Coucky. "But you'll be eating at the table in the house on wheels."

At last she reached the edge of the woods, but a bitter

disappointment was waiting there for her. The merry-go-round, the truck, and the van were gone. There was nothing left of them but a great bare circle under the trees.

Josine wanted to cry but she held her tears back. She saw a man clearing the bank with a sickle in one hand and a forked stick in the other.

"What happened to the merry-go-round?" she asked him.

"Gone," said the man without taking his eyes from the bank. He waved his forked stick down the main road. "Packed up this morning and went down the road."

Josine felt a little better now that she knew in which direction the truck and van had gone. Perhaps the merry-go-round man had moved to a better place down the road. If she walked long enough and far enough, she must surely find him.

She rested awhile under a chestnut tree then continued on the path. Automobiles, motorcycles, and bicycles were racing past. A bicycle went by with two men riding it, the one in back holding his own broken bicycle over his shoulder.

A motor bicycle buzzed past with a man driving it and his wife sitting behind him, holding the baby. A homemade trailer seat on wheels was hooked in back,

75

and two little girls rode in it. They waved to Josine as they went by with their long hair flying in the wind.

A sharp pang of envy pecked at Josine. She wished that she and Coucky could be riding with them. It wouldn't take any time to catch up with the merry-go-round man.

But when she pushed the *poussette* past an automobile parked on the shoulder of the road, she felt better. She looked at the man lying under the car with tools spread within reach of his hand.

"See, Coucky," she said. "You're lucky that you have me instead of an autocar."

At last the path ended and Josine had to push the *poussette* on the pavement. She kept as near the curb as she could. Then she noticed something unusual. There wasn't much traffic on the road any more. It was lined with people standing and watching her push Coucky. A man had even left his horse unhitched in the field while he sat in the grass by the roadside watching the *poussette* go by.

The bright sun had brought drops of perspiration out on Josine's face and made little kiss-curls on her neck and forehead. She was hot and tired, but she tried to look as dignified and grown up as possible since such a crowd had gathered to watch her push Coucky down the road. She wanted them to think that she was his mother.

When a woman called out to her, "My, that's a fine baby you have," she answered in a grown-up way, "Yes, but children can be quite a bother."

Then a line of gaudy two-colored trucks came parading toward them. This must be what the people had come to see. A loud-speaker on a red and black truck told the people that their clothes should be washed with Doit or they wouldn't be clean. A man in a yellow and green truck was throwing paper hats to the bystanders. Josine eagerly held up one hand for a hat. She caught it neatly then unfolded it. Something was written on the hat. Josine was afraid that the writing might be "I will not leave the courtyard without permission." She stopped and asked a woman to read the words for her.

"It says that Alsatian biscuits are the best," said the woman.

Josine was relieved. She put the paper hat on her head and felt as if she were in a Mardi gras parade.

The trucks vanished behind her, but the people still waited at the curbs and crossroads. A man whizzed by on a motorcycle and yelled something to her, but she couldn't hear what he had said.

Then people began shouting at her.

"Look out, little girl!"

"Get out of the way!"

Those who weren't yelling were staring down the road behind her and waving.

Josine looked over her shoulder. She was frightened to see a solid mass of bicycles bearing down upon her and Coucky. Men in striped shirts with their feet strapped to the pedals and their heads low over the handle bars were swooping upon them.

The orpheline started to run. She headed the *poussette* toward the curb but saw that it was too high to be climbed hurriedly. She started to the opposite side, like a hen caught in the same predicament.

"Get out of the road, little girl!" cried someone in the crowd.

"Over here, little one," called someone else.

But another swift glance over her shoulder told Josine that it was too late for that. There was nothing she could do but try to outrun the bicycles. She wildly raced down the road in front of them. The *poussette* clattered, the fringes waved wildly, and Coucky crowed with glee. Her biscuit hat fell off her head and was crushed under a bicycle wheel.

Then Josine's foot struck a stone in the road. She stumbled. As she fell, she let go of the handle. The *poussette* raced a little way by itself.

The bicycles parted into two streams and silently rushed past her. It felt as if the wind was blowing at her from all directions.

When the last bicycle had passed, Josine picked herself up. Her knee was skinned but her first thought was for Coucky.

She saw that a man had run out and was pushing the *poussette* to the side of the road. She limped toward it as fast as her skinned knee would let her.

"Oh, my baby!" she cried. "My poor baby! I wish we had stayed home."

People gathered around the *poussette* and Josine. Then a low-slung car pulled up alongside.

"What's wrong?" asked a man with long black hair. "Were the children hit by the racers?"

"No," panted Josine, "but they fanned us real hard."

Everyone tried to tell him at once what had happened. Josine was not satisfied until she had pulled Coucky into her arms.

"What are you two doing out on the road by yourselves?" asked the long-haired man.

"I didn't want them to take Coucky away from me and put him in the boys' home," said Josine. "I want to take him to the merry-go-round man, but I'm so tired I can't even wiggle my toes. I think I'll take him there tomorrow instead."

The man didn't understand yet.

"Where do you live?" he asked. "Is it near here?"

"We live in a slum with mice and the wall all broken down," said Josine. "The roof almost fell on us one night."

Another man sitting in the back seat with a camera on his knees was impatient. "We better get along, Marcel," he said. "We'll miss the end of the race."

The one called Marcel pulled a notebook out of his pocket. "Armand will be there to cover it," he answered. "This sounds like a good human-interest story. What's your name, little girl?" he asked, poising the pencil.

When Josine saw that he was going to write down what she said, she decided it must be truthful.

"I'm an orpheline," she explained, "and Coucky is really a boy. So they're going to put him in the boys' home. But I don't want him to go there. They beat the boys and don't give them enough to eat."

The man was so interested that Josine answered his questions readily.

"How about a picture to go with the story?" Marcel asked the man with the camera. "Stand here, little girl, and hold the baby in your arms. Move back, everybody!"

Josine obeyed. She liked to have her picture taken, so she smiled as big as her mouth would stretch. Coucky

smiled, too, because he was getting old enough to enjoy hearing voices around him.

"I got it," said the man with the camera. "Let's go on now. I'd like a shot of the finish myself."

But Marcel wouldn't leave until he had found someone to take Josine and Coucky back to the orphanage. He stopped two cars, but one was full of a big family and the other was going to turn off the road at the next crossway.

Then a farmer driving a cartload of manure to his fields stopped his great black horse.

"I'll take the little ones back," he offered. "My farm is on the other side of Ste. Germaine and I pass the orphanage."

Marcel lifted Josine up on the seat beside the farmer. "You go back and rest up," he told Josine. "Leave these big problems to big people."

A man lifted Coucky into Josine's lap.

"Wait! The carriage!" cried a woman.

So the *poussette* was put on top of the farmer's load.

Marcel's car purred as it rolled away. The people went off in all directions toward their homes or their cars. The two-wheeled farm cart slowly creaked down the road.

Josine felt better even if she hadn't found the merry-go-round man. She was sure that Marcel would find him and tell him everything since it was all carefully written down in the notebook. Then the merry-go-round man would come and get Coucky.

She was happy that she would get to keep the baby a little longer anyway. She squeezed him in her arms and looked over the horse's fat back and pointed collar.

"I think this is even grander than the blue coach on the merry-go-round," she told the farmer. "And it doesn't make me sick."

CHAPTER SEVEN

"Where have you been, Josine?" demanded Madame Flattot, who had returned from her visit to Monsieur Roger. "Where did you take Coucky?"

"We were in a bicycle race," explained Josine, "and we almost won, but I fell down."

Madame rolled her eyes up to the heavens then down again to the little orpheline. "You're a naughty, disobedient girl," said Madame. "I don't know what to do with you."

Josine was contrite. "You could pin the signs on me

again," she suggested, because she didn't want anything worse done to her.

The way it ended was that Madame did nothing to Josine. The whole affair had left her so speechless that she decided not to speak to Josine or pay her any attention.

"No one shall speak to her for a week," decided Madame Flattot.

This made Josine feel worse than if she had been given one of the spankings that was out of style.

But Brigitte whispered to her as they undressed for bed that night, "Don't feel too bad, dear. They'll start talking to you soon. They won't be able to stay mad for a whole week."

Josine herself could still talk to Coucky. She ran to his crib and leaned over him. "Never mind, Coucky," she told him. "The merry-go-round man will come to get you soon. And maybe he'll adopt me. Nobody loves us any more."

But the very next day everyone began talking to Josine again.

Genevieve returned from the grocery store during the two-hour dinner period. She was clutching a newspaper in her hand. Her face was so white that her freckles looked like cinnamon. She could hardly speak sensibly.

"It's awful," she cried, waving the newspaper at Madame Flattot. "It's terrible!"

Madame's face went white as Genevieve's. "Is it war?" she cried.

"No, no," answered Genevieve, thrusting the newspaper into her hands. "It's worse. It's Josine."

Madame Flattot straightened the paper before her eyes. All the orphelines tried to look at it through her arms. Marie pulled at her left arm and Yvette at her right. The paper was nearly torn in two.

"A picture of Josine and Coucky!" exclaimed Madame Flattot in surprise. "Right on the front page of the *Paris Morning*."

Josine tried to see it, too. She thrust her head between Madame's arms. It really was a picture of her and Coucky. There was a broad grin on her face and an angel smile on Coucky's.

"A man took it," said Josine. "Perhaps we really did win the race."

Then Madame Flattot's eyes split open as she read the caption under the picture. Her lips slowly made the printed letters into spoken words. "Must these sad waifs be parted?" she read the big print.

Everyone was astounded.

"I'm not a waif," said Josine indignantly. She didn't

86

know what it meant, but the French word for it had a dismal sound.

The other orphelines were even more indignant.

"If you hadn't run off without permission," said Brigitte, "you wouldn't be one."

"And you've made Coucky a waif, too," scolded Marie.

"You've probably made all of us waifs," accused Yvette.

Madame Flattot read the article under the picture. As she read it aloud, her voice grew higher and the words came faster. She left out many parts in her haste to get to the end.

"Poor abandoned children living in a slum with a leaky roof and broken wall," she read. "Mice may cause epidemic. . . . Where is our public conscience? . . . Conditions in boys' orphanage even worse. Must this tiny waif be torn from his foster sister's arms and condemned to grow up with rats and toads? The plight of these unfortunate orphans is a disgrace to France," ended Madame.

The orphelines looked at Josine with fresh ire.

"You've even disgraced our mother France," said Yvette in a shocked voice.

Madame Flattot sank into a chair. She leaned back,

her feet spread out in front of her with the toes turned up. The newspaper dropped from her hand. For a few minutes, she could only close her eyes and groan.

"Our shame is held up for all Paris to see," she said at last.

Genevieve was no consolation. "Everyone in the village is talking about it," she said.

Brigitte had picked the newspaper off the floor. "Let's frame the picture of Josine and Coucky and hang it in the parlor," she suggested. "We can cut the waifs off the bottom."

No one paid any attention to her.

"My work with children is ended," moaned Madame. "Who would hire me to care for them now? I will have to go back to cooking at the inn."

Genevieve was worried, too. "They say that the president of the Republic should investigate it himself," she said.

"Will we get to see him?" asked Brigitte eagerly.

Still no one paid any attention to her.

"I'm going upstairs and pack my suitcase," said Genevieve. "They will surely dismiss me, because the children were in my care yesterday afternoon. I will have to marry that stupid Jacques my godmother is saving for me."

The harsh jangle of the gate bell made everyone jump.

"It's the president," cried Brigitte. "He's here already."

"No," cried Josine. "It's the merry-go-round man. He's come for me and Coucky."

Genevieve was frightened. "I'm not going to open the gate," she announced. "I'm going upstairs and start packing."

Madame Flattot rose majestically from her chair. She

lifted her head proudly. "It is the end," she announced. "All we need is courage."

She walked through the door like an aristocrat going to the guillotine in old France. "I have nothing but my life to lose," she said. Then her courage left her. "And twenty little girls and one little boy I have loved like my own." She burst into noisy tears.

It was Brigitte who finally opened the gate.

Monsieur de Goupil rushed through it. He, too, was carrying the morning newspaper in his hand and he was quivering with excitement.

He shook the paper at Madame Flattot.

"Ah, the newspapers are beginning to print the truth," he cried.

Madame Flattot stared at him through dim eyes. "Is that the *Paris Morning?*" she asked in bewilderment. "Have you read it?"

"Indeed I have," gloated Monsieur de Goupil. "And so have those directors. I can tell you they have kept my telephone ringing. Ah, it is a great victory, Madame."

"Did you read the *front* page?" asked Madame Flattot, because she thought that surely Monsieur was talking about some sporting event.

"Everyone in Paris has read it," said Monsieur de Goupil. "There is no power like that of the press—and a persistent child."

Madame Flattot spoke bluntly. "Why have you come here, Monsieur?" she asked.

But he only gave her an arch glance and asked a question himself.

"Madame," he asked, "how would you like to be the mother of thirty-one boys as well as twenty girls?"

"You are joking, Monsieur," said Madame in a trembling voice. "It is very unkind."

Monsieur de Goupil looked hurt. "I was never more serious," he answered. "Josine's interview with the press made the directors change their minds about my brilliant idea."

Madame fastened her eyes on him. "Just what *is* your brilliant idea, Monsieur?" she asked point-blank.

"To combine the orphanages," he answered. "For months I have been working on those stubborn directors." He looked for Josine among the children and patted her curly head. "It has taken a child to convince them that I was right," he explained.

Madame Flattot had a hard time getting used to Monsieur's words.

"And where will we all live together?" she asked. "In this broken-down house or in their broken-down one?"

Monsieur jokingly shook his finger at her. "Tatata, Madame," he chided her, "you have no imagination such as mine. It has been decided that we will buy a large property in the country." He looked at the goggling orphelines. "How would you like to live in a real castle?" he asked them. "With its own garden and woods."

"With Coucky?" asked Josine. Now that people had begun talking to her again, they were saying such surprising things.

"With Coucky and thirty other boys," said Monsieur. "The boys will have one wing and the girls the other. And of course you and Genevieve will have more help," he assured Madame Flattot.

"Does it have towers and a secret stairway?" asked Brigitte.

"And a moat?" asked Yvette.

"Of course it has all those things," said Monsieur de Goupil. "It has been in the hands of a proud and noble family for hundreds of years."

Madame Flattot was beginning to grasp the situation. "You mean it is even older than this house?" she asked suspiciously.

"Madame," said Monsieur de Goupil reprovingly, "it is a *castle*. This place is a slum."

Madame tried to reason this out but gave up. "How soon will we move?" she asked.

Monsieur looked around uneasily. "It will be a few months yet," he said. "Maybe not until next spring.

Plumbing will have to be installed in the castle and many of the windows need panes to keep the bats out. And of course the moat will have to be drained to make it safe for children. That will get rid of the mosquitoes, too." He dropped his eyes before Madame's straightforward stare. "My brother-in-law, the Duke, hasn't lived in it for ten years," he explained, "so it needs a few repairs."

The orphelines did not care if the castle was in ruins.

"We'll get to have Coucky with us always," cried Josine with delight. "And we can play marbles with those other boys."

Madame Flattot burst into tears again, but they were caused by joy. "Thirty-one boys and twenty girls," she repeated. "When I was first married, I prayed God for children, but He didn't give me any. Now He is sending them to me in droves." She rubbed her eyes. "Well, we mustn't be fussy about the way our prayers are answered," she added briskly.

"What about Coucky?" asked Josine. "Are you going to take him to the boys' home today?"

"You may as well keep him on here," said Monsieur de Goupil. "It will be a good way for you to get used to boys."

"I'm used to them already," said Josine, "but they aren't used to me yet."

93

Then Monsieur de Goupil took her hand in his, bowed, and kissed it as if she were a big married woman.

"You have a strong character, Josine," he said, "with remarkable tenacity. You are a credit to Madame's upbringing."

"Am I really?" asked Josine proudly, although she didn't know what all that meant. "Everybody else says I'm stubborn."

Long after Monsieur de Goupil had driven away in high good humor, Madame Flattot and Genevieve and the orphelines talked about the great change which was to come into their lives.

"If anyone were to ask my opinion," said Madame to Genevieve, "I would have to say truthfully that I think Monsieur's brilliant idea was how to help his brother-in-law sell his old run-down castle." Genevieve agreed with her. "And if anyone were to ask my opinion about Coucky," continued Madame, "I would have to answer truthfully that I have been thinking for some time that one of those Arab workmen left him in the basket."

"Probably the one who went back to Africa," said Genevieve. "His hair is really too curly for a gypsy's."

Madame Flattot noticed the children listening to them with rounded eyes and lips.

"Now not a word of this to anyone, girls," she cautioned. "We purse our lips so, put a little key in them so, turn the key so—then throw it away."

All the children put imaginary keys to their pursed lips, locked them, and threw the keys away. All but Josine. "I'm going to put my key in my pocket," she said. "I might meet that man who made us waifs again."

"Heaven forbid!" hoped Madame Flattot.

Then they all began to talk at once about the castle in the country.

"We can play we are queens and princesses," said Brigitte.

"And explore the towers and the woods," added Yvette.

"And we'll have thirty-one brothers," said Marie. "They can be our knights."

Yvette wasn't sure that it would be a good thing to have so many brothers. "Suppose they don't like us," she said. "Perhaps our knights will throw rocks at us and chase us with lizards."

But Josine was not worried about that. "I'm not afraid of boys," she boasted. "They're just Couckys grown up bigger."

About the author . . .

NATALIE SAVAGE CARLSON was born in Winchester, Virginia, one of a family of seven girls and a boy. She spent most of her childhood on a farm in Maryland, amid an atmosphere reminiscent of the circus. Her father, a circus enthusiast, trained his children to perform on the trapeze, the tightrope, and on horseback, two of the horses having been purchased from a circus. In between kitchen chores, the family cook liked to perform stunts on a barrel.

When Mrs. Carlson was eleven, the family moved to Long Beach, California, where she attended Polytechnic High and St. Anthony's. She also studied at U.C.L.A., and was a reporter on the *Long Beach Sun* for two years.

Mrs. Carlson is married to a naval officer and has traveled extensively. She was in Honolulu at the time of Pearl Harbor, and has also lived in San Diego, California; Seattle; Oregon; Michigan; Nebraska; Oklahoma; Connecticut; and Rhode Island. She recently returned from a lengthy stay in Paris, France, where her husband was assigned to duty and where she met the children who inspired this book and THE HAPPY ORPHELINE. She now lives in Newport, Rhode Island.

Mrs. Carlson and her husband have two daughters and a granddaughter.

A number of Mrs. Carlson's stories have appeared in magazines for children. Her books include: THE TALKING CAT, WINGS AGAINST THE WIND, SASHES RED AND BLUE, THE FAMILY UNDER THE BRIDGE, and, of course, the two books about the lovable little French orphans, THE HAPPY ORPHELINE and A BROTHER FOR THE ORPHELINES.

About the artist . . .

GARTH WILLIAMS was born in New York City, of parents who were both artists. He was educated in England, and was graduated from the Royal College of Art in London. He later spent considerable time in many of the large capitals of Europe. In 1936 he won the British Prix de Rome for sculpture.

During World War II, Mr. Williams served with the British Red Cross in London.

Mr. Williams now lives in Aspen, Colorado, with his wife and two daughters, and devotes most of his time to illustrating books for children. Among the books he has illustrated are: THE TALL BOOK OF MAKE-BELIEVE; E. B. White's STUART LITTLE and CHARLOTTE'S WEB;

the new edition of the Laura Ingalls Wilder "Little House" books; LITTLE FUR FAMILY, WAIT TILL THE MOON IS FULL, and THREE LITTLE ANIMALS, by Margaret Wise Brown; THE GOLDEN NAME DAY, by Jennie D. Lindquist; and Mrs. Carlson's THE HAPPY ORPHELINE and THE FAMILY UNDER THE BRIDGE. He both wrote and illustrated THE ADVENTURES OF BENJAMIN PINK and THE RABBITS' WEDDING.